The Grizzly Bear's Eyelash

T. Jacira Paolino

ISBN: 978-1-4834-3993-8 (sc)
ISBN: 978-1-4834-3994-5 (hc)
ISBN: 978-1-4834-3992-1 (e)

Library of Congress Control Number: 2015916752

Illustrations: Alice Brake
Editor: Barbara Riley

Author's picture by Donald P. Paolino
Illustrator's picture by T. Jacira Paolino

Lulu Publishing Services rev. date: 9/8/2016

To all the veterans
who return from war to their families,
Thank you for your service.

To my children and grandchildren, may
you always have patience and kindness.

And finally, to Silvano Toso,
a special thank you,
for without your help, this book
would never have been possible.

**Please do NOT attempt
to pet a wild grizzly bear.**

**This story is a fable.
Wild animals are very dangerous!**

The rain was pounding down from the heavens the night a young woman named Miyaku appeared on the doorstep of the village witch's home. Fearfully, she raised her hand and knocked on the door.

Almost immediately, the door began to slowly swing open, and the witch stood there with a smile on her face.

"I knew you would come," she said. "Please come in."

Miyaku stepped inside out of the rain. She found herself in a cozy living room with a blazing fireplace. In front of the fireplace were two comfortable rocking chairs. The witch sat down in one and, with a gesture, invited Miyaku to sit in the other.

"How can I help you?" asked the witch.

As she took her seat, Miyaku felt the tears well up in her eyes.

"I need you to make me a magic potion," said Miyaku. "My husband hasn't been himself ever since he came home from the war. He used to be so patient, loving, and attentive, but now he is distant and cold and sometimes angry. Instead of going to work, he sits on the balcony staring out at the sea."

"If I ask him a question, he snaps at me, and if the food I serve isn't just to his liking, he shoves it aside without eating it. I want you to make him a potion that will turn him back the way he used to be. Please!" Miyaku pleaded.

The witch breathed a deep sigh and stared into the fire for what seemed like forever. Finally, she slowly turned her head to Miyaku and said, "It is often this way with men after they return from war. I will make you the magic potion, but there is one special ingredient I need you to find for me. You must bring me a freshly plucked eyelash from a grizzly bear, and you must pluck it yourself. It cannot be one that has naturally fallen out."

Miyaku's hopes were dashed. How would she ever be able to get an eyelash from a live grizzly bear without being shredded to smithereens by his razor-sharp claws?

Dejectedly, she rose from the rocking chair and headed toward the door. With her hand on the doorknob, she turned and said to the witch, "I don't know how, but I will try to get the eyelash."

The very next night, Miyaku took a bowl of meat out into the woods near a cave. She knew a bear lived there. She kept a safe distance, and when the bear came out and cautiously sniffed the air, attracted by the scent of the meat, she set the bowl down on the ground, turned, and calmly walked back down the mountain to her home.

The next night, she returned, only she walked a few steps closer. Again, when the bear came out, she set the meat down on the ground, turned, and left.

She repeated this for several weeks, gradually getting closer to the bear until the bear was no longer startled but rather accustomed to her approaching him every night.

One night, she got close enough to give the meat to the bear.

She stayed very still while he ate. Then when the bear was done, she took her bowl, turned around, and left.

For several more nights, she just watched the bear eat. Then one night, she waited until the bear was done eating, and she gently stroked his head before taking the bowl and turning to leave.

In the following weeks, she began talking to the bear in a calm and soothing voice while she continued to stroke his head. She would tell the bear how her husband used to be before he went away to the war, how he would hug her as she stood at the kitchen sink doing dishes after dinner, or how he would stroke her hair as she sat in her favorite armchair reading a book.

Then one night, she softly spoke to the bear and explained that she needed one of his eyelashes. He seemed to almost comprehend what she was saying.

After he finished eating, he semi-closed his eyes and leaned forward with his head toward Miyaku and waited. Ever so gently, she pinched an eyelash between her fingertips and tugged.

The bear allowed her to do that. She took the eyelash and ran all the way to the witch's house.

Excitedly, she knocked on the door, and when the witch opened it, she proudly showed her the eyelash. "Look!" said Miyaku. "I got it!"

The witch took the eyelash and held it up to the light. Then she walked across the living room and threw the eyelash into the fire.

"What are you doing?" shouted Miyaku.

"Tell me how you got the eyelash!" demanded the witch.

"Well, I went to the woods every night with a bowl of meat. Each night I got closer and closer. Finally, the bear trusted me enough to eat it while I held the bowl, and after many nights, he let me stroke his head. Sometimes he would make a contented sound with his throat. I would talk to him so he got used to my voice, and after a very long time, I asked permission and he allowed me to pluck the eyelash."

"Yes, exactly, you tamed the bear and won his confidence and love," said the witch.

"But it was all for nothing! You threw the eyelash in the fire!"

"No, it was not all for nothing because the eyelash is no longer needed, nor do you need the potion. Miyaku, let me ask you something. Is a man more ferocious than a bear? Is he less responsive to kindness and understanding? If you can win the love and confidence of a wild, blood-thirsty beast, surely you can do the same with your husband."

Miyaku stood motionless for a few moments. Then she turned to run back home to her husband. Stopping at the door of the witch's house, she said with a huge smile, "Thank you!"

And the moral of this story is that you can tame any kind of wild beast—even human— with patience, love, kindness, ... and food!

The Grizzly Bear's Eyelash
Discussion Topics

Why does Miyaku want to change her husband back to how he was before the war?

What do you think happened to her husband to cause him to change the way he behaves?

What is a witch?

Is there such a thing as a good witch, and if so, where did that concept come from?

A stereotypical witch with a black pointy hat and a broomstick to fly on isn't at all how the witch in this story looks. How do you expect a witch to look? Why do we expect a witch to look a certain way?

Do you think the witch's home looks like anyone else's home in the village? Why or why not?

Why did the author choose an eyelash as the necessary ingredient in the magic potion and not a claw, or tooth, or lock of fur?

What motivated the wife to take such risk to get near the grizzly bear?

Would you take a risk like that under the same circumstances? Why or why not?

What is the correlation between the grizzly bear and the husband, if any?

Post-Traumatic Stress Syndrome is common among people coming home from war. What are some of the symptoms of PTSD?

What can we do to help our soldiers adjust to re-entry into society after their experience in military service?

The Grizzly Bear has been on the endangered species list in the USA since 1975, but there is a proposal to take them off the list in 2016. Should grizzly bears still be protected?

**Please tell anyone you know who may be
dealing with PTSD about this book.
10% of the profits from the sale of this book will
be donated to help veterans' organizations.**

About the Author:

T. Jacira Paolino (formerly Castro) is a polyglot with a BA in Modern Languages and an MA in Information Technology. She has lived in the United States, Mexico, Ecuador, Chile, Italy, and the United Kingdom.
She is a simultaneous interpreter and technical translator as well as a multilingual web developer. She has two children, Avelina and Pablo, and two grandchildren, Breck and Sierra. She resides in south Florida.

About the Illustrator:

Alice Brake was 14 years old when she illustrated this book! She grew up in Spain but now lives in central Florida with her parents and her younger brother. She has a great love for reading and drawing and is a math whiz. She hopes to one day
be an author and an English teacher. She is extremely honored to be a part of this story.

About the Story:

This story, originally published by Ms. Paolino in Italian and entitled, *La storia della ciglia dell'orso grizzly*, won the silver award (second place) in the XXIV National 50 & Più competition for prose held in the city of Levico Terme, Trentino, Italy, in 2006.